Published 1992 by **Thomasson-Grant, Inc.**
Copyright ©1992 Editions Dessain, Liege.
Original title: *Petites Histoires*.
This book, or any portions thereof,
may not be reproduced in any form
without written permission from the publisher.
Printed in Belgium.
99 98 97 96 95 94 93 92   5 4 3 2 1

Library of Congress Cataloging-in-Publication Data

Brouillard, Anne.
   [Petites histoires. English]
   Three topsy-turvy tales / Anne Brouillard.
      p.   cm.
   Translation of: Petites histoires.
   Summary: In three wordless episodes, animal friends
      endure life's surprises together.
   ISBN 1-56566-017-X
   [1. Animals—Fiction. 2. Friendship—Fiction.
    3. Stories without words.] I. Title.
   PZ7.B79975Ti 1992   92-5445
   [E]—dc20   CIP
                                                   AC

Thomasson-Grant
One Morton Drive
Charlottesville, VA 22901
(804) 977-1780

Anne Brouillard

Three Topsy~Turvy Tales

Thomasson-Grant
Charlottesville, Virginia

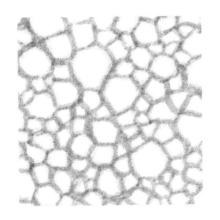

Snowfall Downfall

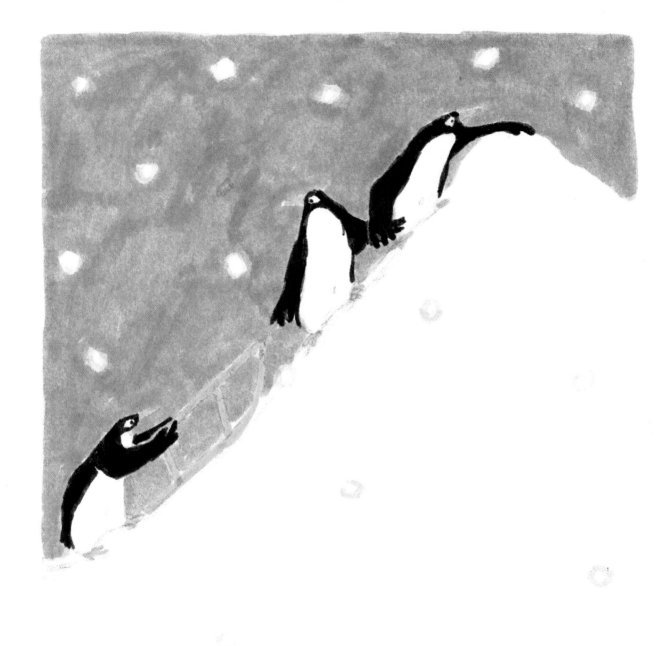

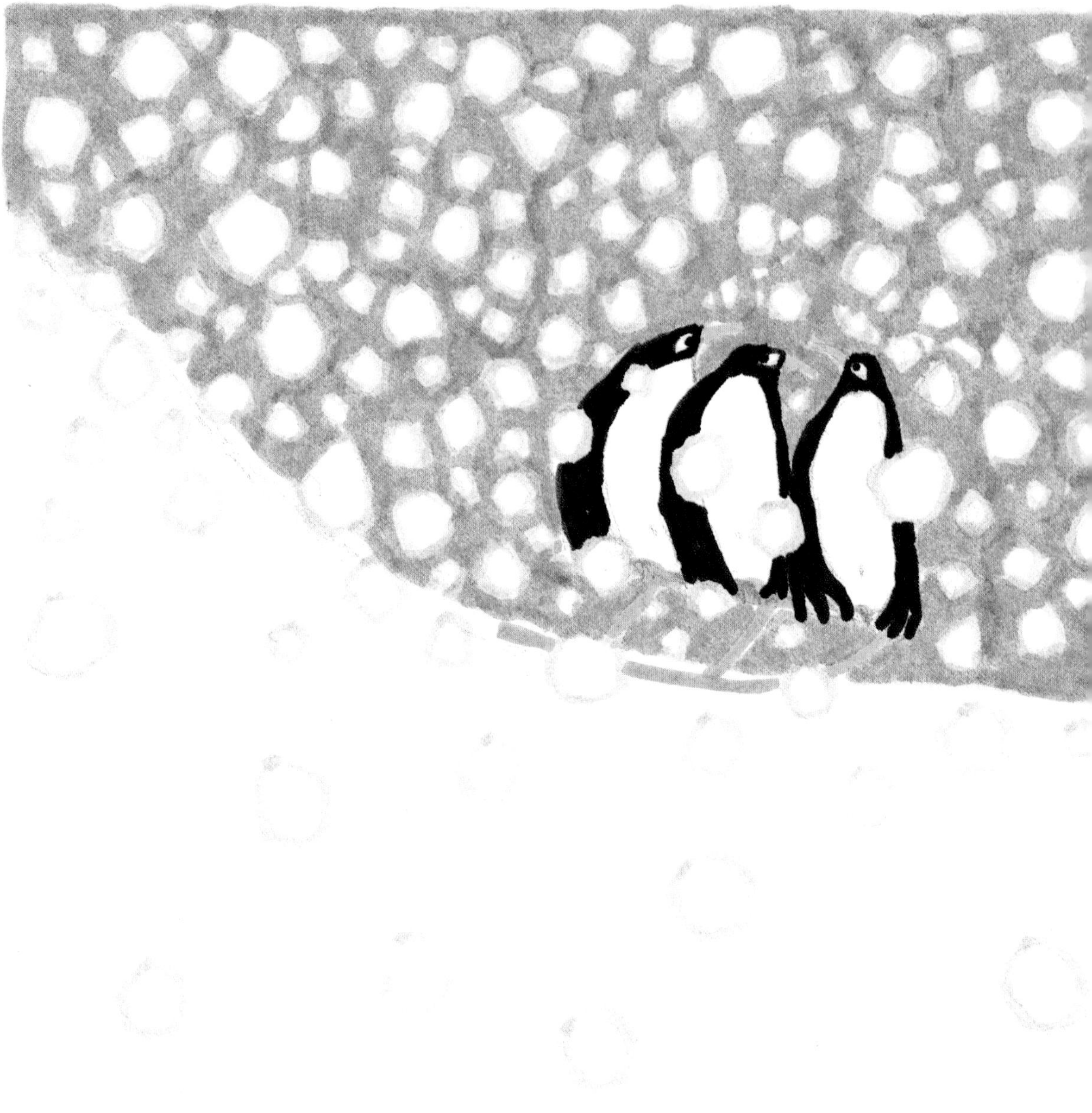

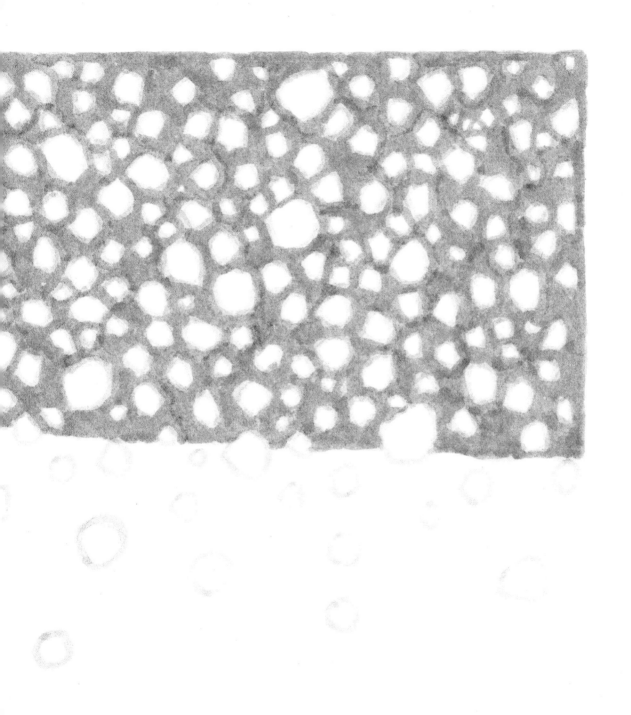

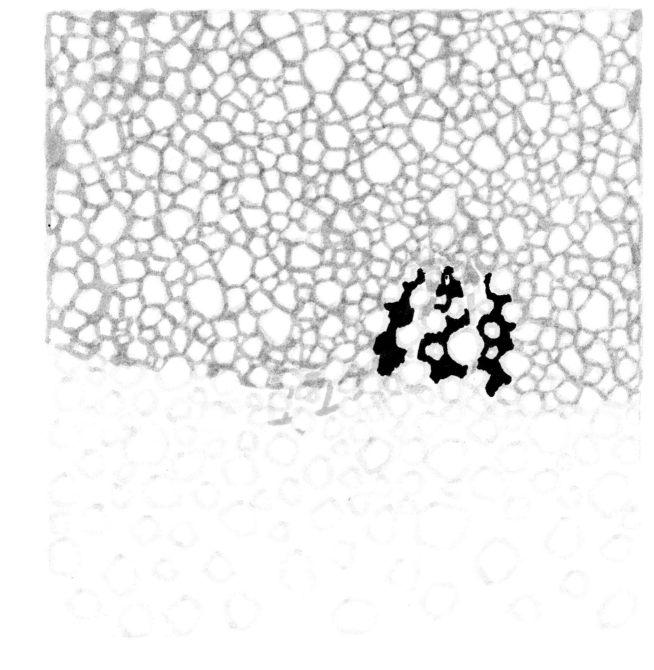

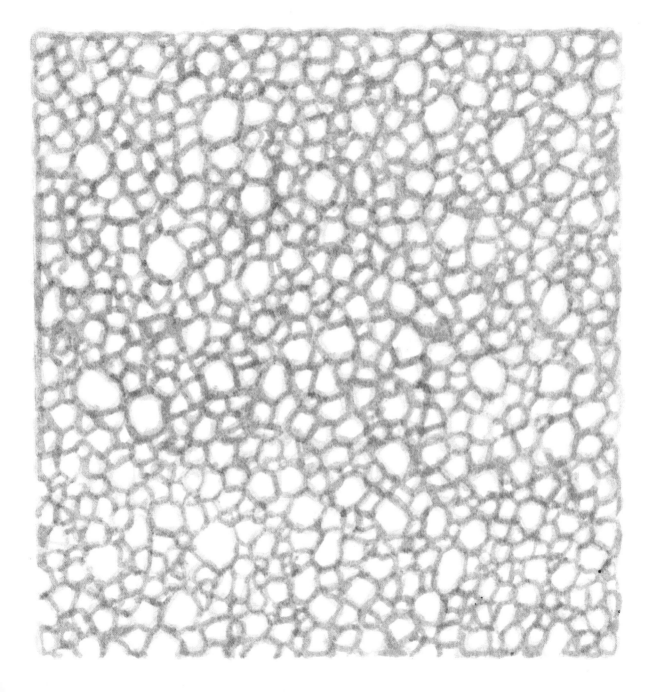

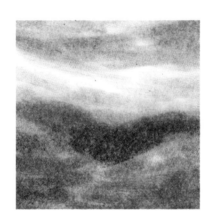

Upside Downpour

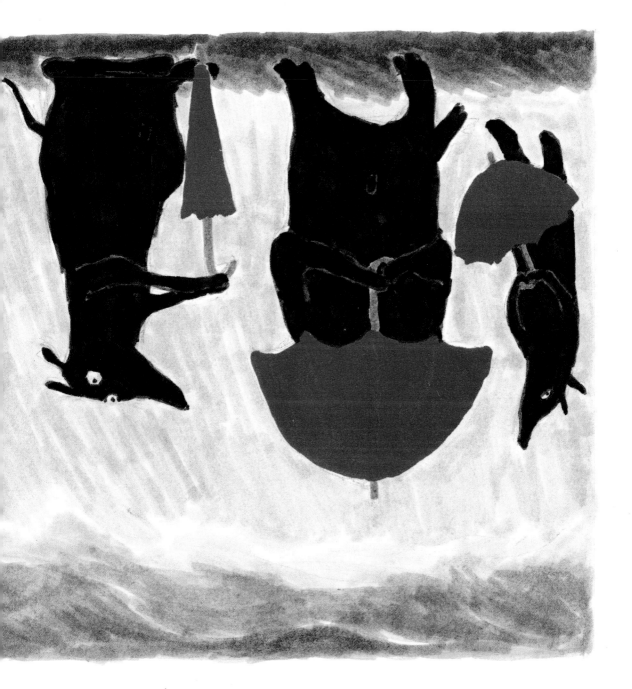

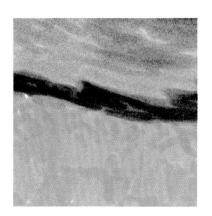

Swingset Upset

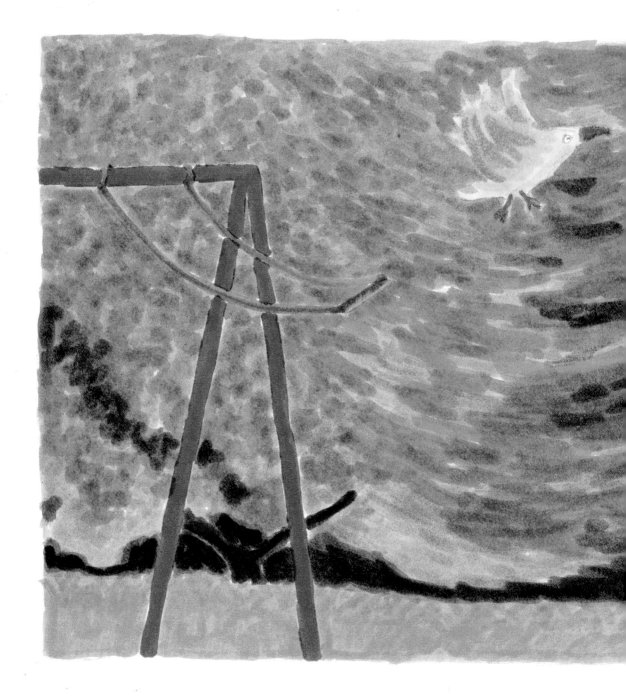

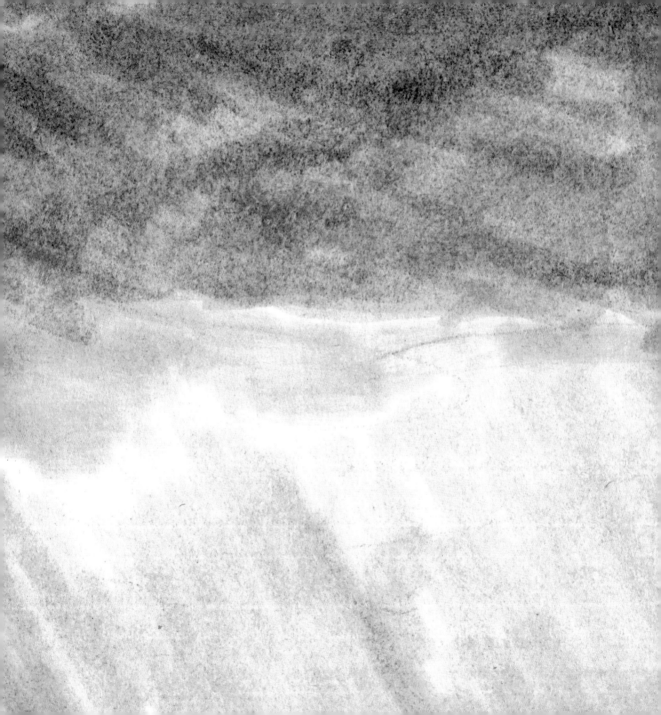